Rachel
A MIGHTY BIG
IMAGINING
LYNNE KOSITSKY

Rachel
A MIGHTY BIG
IMAGINING
LYNNE KOSITSKY

Penguin Books

PENGUIN BOOKS

Published by the Penguin Group

Penguin Books Canada Ltd, 10 Alcorn Avenue, Toronto, Ontario, Canada M4V 3B2

Penguin Books Ltd, 27 Wrights Lane, London W8 5TZ, England

Penguin Putnam Inc., 375 Hudson Street, New York, New York 10014, U.S.A

Penguin Books Australia Ltd, Ringwood, Victoria, Australia

Penguin Books (NZ) Ltd, cnr Rosedale and Airborne Roads, Albany, Auckland 1310, New Zealand

Penguin Books Ltd, Registered Offices: Harmondsworth, Middlesex, England

DESIGN: MATTHEWS COMMUNICATIONS DESIGN INC.

MAP ILLUSTRATION: SHARON MATTHEWS

INTERIOR ILLUSTRATIONS: RON LIGHTBURN

First published, 2001

1   3   5   7   9   10   8   6   4   2

Copyright © Lynne Kositsky, 2001

Manufactured in Canada

National Library of Canada Cataloguing in Publication Data

Kositsky, Lynne, 1947-

A mighty big imagining : Rachel

(Our Canadian girl)

ISBN 0-14-100252-2

1. Freedmen—Nova Scotia —Juvenile fiction.
2. Slavery—Emancipation—Juvenile fiction. I. Title. II. Series.

PS8571.O85M54 2001   jC813'.54   C2001-901160-1

PZ7.K85254Mi 2001

Visit Penguin Canada's website at **www.penguin.ca**

For my children

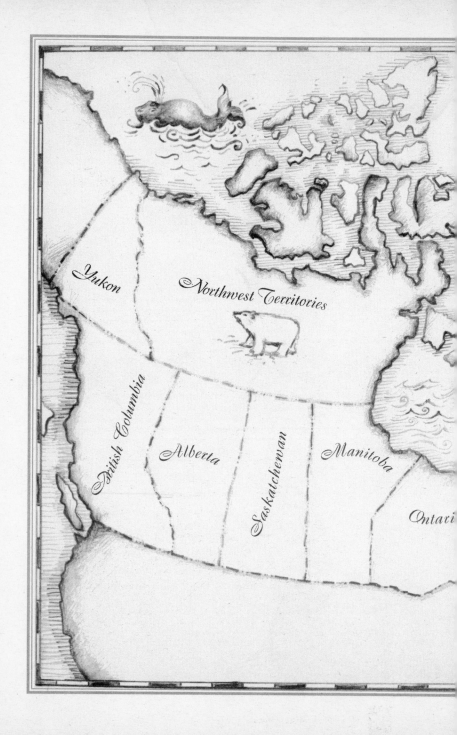

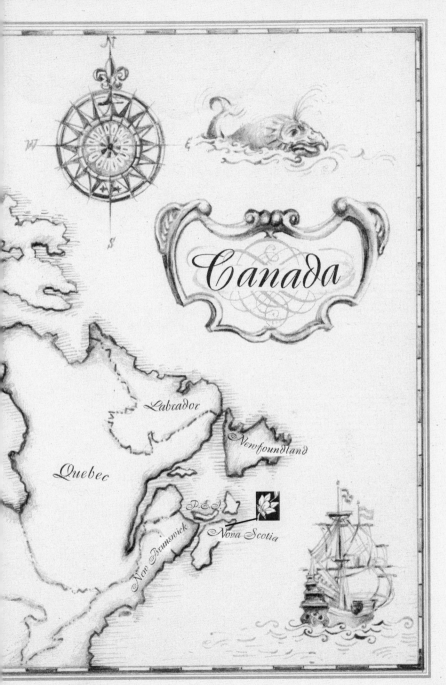

Canada

Labrador

Newfoundland

Quebec

P.E.I.

Nova Scotia

New Brunswick

 Marks the location of the story

MEET RACHEL

I T IS HARD ENOUGH TO IMAGINE LIFE WITHOUT TV, electricity, or running water. Now try to picture living without enough food or clothing, without a comfortable home or medicine. This is the world that Rachel, a slave girl of the eighteenth century, was born into.

Rachel grew up near Charlestown, in South Carolina, where at least two-thirds of the population were slaves. Rachel's grandmother was kidnapped by slave traders and brought over from West Africa, together with many other black people. All were forced to stay in the British colony, living in terrible conditions.

The year our story takes place is 1783, and most of the descendants of these original slaves now work in the rice fields of the plantations, planting and picking the rice known as "Carolina gold." It's a harsh and thankless life, and many die before their time.

In a sense Rachel and her mother were lucky during their years on the plantation. They were house slaves and did not have to work outside in the searing heat. But although the master and mistress were wealthy, with beautiful clothes and sumptuous food, Rachel was dressed in thin rags made of a poor cloth reserved for slaves, and was only ever given rice to eat, the spoiled or broken grains that were not good enough to sell. If she became sick on this diet, she could only get better or die. The master and mistress did not want to spend money on doctors for slaves because they were easily replaced. The mistress was also quick to punish Rachel with a severe beating if she misbehaved.

While Rachel was still a very small child, tension between Britain and her thirteen American colonies grew. The colonists, including Rachel's master, were angry that they were being taxed so heavily, and that Britain had so much control over them. In 1776, after several small clashes, a war called the American Revolution broke out between the colonies and Britain. Almost everybody took sides. Rachel's master supported the Revolution. He was called a Patriot. But some people, the Loyalists, remained loyal to Britain and the English king. They fought on the side of the British army and if caught would often be subjected to the humiliating and dangerous punishment of being covered in hot tar and feathers.

The slaves on Rachel's plantation were caught in the middle. But the British promised them their freedom if they escaped their Patriot owners and fought as Loyalists. Rachel, her mother, and her stepfather decided to run away to the British, and although they did not engage in the fighting, they worked with the soldiers and their wives, setting up camps, cooking, sewing, and washing. When the British lost the war, Rachel's family were afraid that they would be sent back to their owners. The British, however, offered them certificates to show they were free.

By the late fall of 1783, Rachel's stepfather has already been shipped from the port of New York to another British colony, Nova Scotia, while Rachel and her mother wait at the docks, eager to join him.

RUN AWAY from my plantation, near Charlestown by the Cooper River. Three Negroes, my property, going by the names of Titan, Sukey, and Rachel. All speak good English.

Titan, a pretty tall fellow with two toes missing had on when he went away Negro cloth jacket and britches.

Sukey, a thin woman with a scar on the left forehead, had on Negro cloth dress and loose shoes.

Rachel, a very black young girl, straight limbed, daughter of Sukey, had on Negro cloth skirt, shift, no shoes. Took their blankets with them, and an axe. It is thought they may try to join up with the King's forces.

Whoever delivers the said Negroes, any or all of them, to me, Joshua Roberts, at my plantation, or to the work-house at Charlestown, shall receive Ten Pounds currency reward for the fellow, Five Pounds for the woman, Three Pounds for the girl.

CHAPTER N° 1

"Boats are bad," Mamma had always said. "They take you from your own place, where you belong, to a country far, far across the sea where you mus' slave for a cruel white missus and massa." All the more remarkable, then, that Mamma and Rachel were now standing on the deck of a great ship in the New York harbour, wishing to sail away on it.

"Name?" the Englishman in charge demanded of Mamma. Seated at a desk in the middle of the scrubbed deck, he stared at her quizzically before dipping his quill in ink and holding it poised above his book.

Mamma grasped Rachel's wrist so hard her icy fingers left a pale fingerprint bracelet on her daughter's dark skin. It looked as though she were afraid that Rachel, if released, might run away. But Rachel knew better. Mamma, usually so brave and so bossy, was scared as a cat-trapped mouse and grabbing hold of her for comfort. Mamma was terrified of white people.

"Name?" the man repeated, clearly annoyed.

Rachel glanced behind her. There were at least forty more Negroes waiting in line behind them, thinly clothed and almost dancing with cold on the wind-swept deck. This man probably wanted to be through with his accounting of them so he could get to his hot meal and bed.

"Sukey, suh. And this here's my daughter Rachel."

"Sukey what?"

"Don' have no last name, suh," Mamma mumbled, staring down at the tummy bump of her soon-to-be baby. She was still clutching Rachel's wrist for dear life.

"Were you slaves?"

"Yessuh, the both of us, at Massa Roberts' rice plantation near Charlestown."

"You can take his surname, then. I'll put you down as Sukey and Rachel Roberts." He wrote rapidly.

A little brown bird landed on the deck and hopped towards Rachel.

"If you please, suh . . ." murmured Rachel. She could just make out a very large R and very small O on the yellow paper. Although she couldn't read, she knew the shapes of some of the letters. She'd seen the missus write in her journal often enough.

"Yes, what is it?"

"We don't want his name. He never did anything for us. He only whipped us and called us bad Nigras. We don't want any reminders of him at all. If it please you . . ."

"Well?" A tiny teardrop of ink splashed from

the man's waiting pen onto the page.

Rachel glanced at the bird before saying firmly, "Our name is Sparrow. Sukey and Rachel Sparrow."

Mamma sighed in surprise.

"Sparrow be it, then." The man crossed out the R and O and wrote something else in their place. Rachel watched intently. Tossing back his mane of white hair, the man looked at her properly for the first time, as if she were a grown-up. "Your ages?"

"I'm around ten, I'm almost sure. I remember the siege of Charlestown, the terrible noise and fear of it. And Mamma's going on thirty."

"You speak very good English, girl." The man actually smiled, and his face creased like starched linen.

"I was a house slave, suh. I copied the missus, the way she spoke. Then, when we escaped, I copied the soldiers' wives."

"Good for you." A make-believe iron smoothed out his smile, and he went on with his writing.

"Where we goin', suh?" Mamma asked timidly, afraid to interrupt his work.

"To Shelburne, Port Roseway, in Nova Scotia, woman, to a new, free life. Didn't anybody tell you?"

"Oh, yessuh. I jus' wanted to make sure they were right. You see, my husband, Titan, who works for the army, he's on another boat. He's gone before to put up wood houses for the settlers. We wouldn' want to end up someplace else."

"You shall not, I promise you."

"Can we stay on board tonight, suh? We're afraid to go on shore, afraid the massa will find us and drag us back." That was the talk all over town: the slave owners were coming to claim their property now the war was ended. The scar above Mamma's eyebrow seemed to blaze out now, a lick of crimson paint on her brown skin.

"You may. We'll be turning no one away. We sail on the morning tide."

The man waved his hand to dismiss them and gazed at the ocean till his eyes turned the same glass grey as the winter shimmer of water.

"Sukey and Rachel Sparrow, free Nigras in Nova Scotia," Mamma whispered as they climbed below. She'd let go of Rachel at last. "I jus' love the sound of that. Here's your blanket, girl. Gird it round you to stop your shiverin', and never mind the holes."

Rachel nodded. Free Nigras. She didn't even know what that meant. No massa to yell at her, perhaps, and no missus to pull her hair. If she were really lucky, there might even be enough to eat. She thought of all the food on the missus' table in Charlestown and imagined herself stuffing it into her own hungry mouth. That was a mighty big imagining, and she sighed at the effort, pulling her threadbare blanket round her. It was awfully cold up here. She'd never suffered such cold. Even the wild, wet heat of summer on the plantation, with the mosquitoes stinging her skin raw, was better than this. She began the slippery climb down to the ship's hold, hoping the future would be more to her liking than the past.

CHAPTER N°2

"When will we be there?" Rachel demanded of Mamma. "Has Titan built a house for us? Will it shelter us from the cold?"

They had left port several days before, escorted by a British warship, but their boat had been becalmed for a long time, swaying and dipping in tiny eddies of water. Rachel had begun to think that she'd never see Nova Scotia. Then the winds had picked up, icy and bitter, and sleet had begun to drive at them in a fierce arc. The sails had filled with gusty air and damp, and the boat had groaned, shaking itself like a giant sea creature. Soon it had begun to move again.

Mamma smiled wanly. She was sick to her stomach from the lurching of the ship and the new baby inside her. "Hush," was all she said. "We'll know when we know, and there ain't no use a-frettin' about it."

"I want to know now. I want this trip to end, and for us to be off the boat."

"Trip is jus' an arm long, you can reach clean across it," declared Mamma in that mysterious way of hers, and there was suddenly no more to be said. No more, that is, until a strange ship was sighted in the distance.

"What's that?" shouted Mamma, her fearful voice flying off into the gale.

"I heard someone say it's a privateer, Mamma, a rebel ship, ready to board us. See how close it comes. At least there's no cargo here that could possibly be worth its while."

"No cargo?" broke in a Negro man who was standing alongside of them. "No cargo, hey?

We're the cargo. It'll take us back south and sell us off as slaves."

Mamma's lips went white as pine ash. Rachel, too, felt the blood wash out of her face. To come so far, only to be dragged back. It was unbearable. But as she cuddled close to Mamma, her chin wobbling, her knees weak as cotton, the British warship protecting them fired one warning shot. Rachel and Mamma jumped back as though hit. The rebel boat came no closer. Instead, it shortened its sails and turned away, facing the wind. Soon, to their relief, they had left it far behind, a speck, then a glint, then nothing on the pale horizon.

Rachel thought she'd never feel entirely safe again.

Two days later they sailed into an eerie fog. It muffled the noise of sea and gulls completely. Every creak and cry of the ship sounded as loud as a pistol crack and set their hearts to hammering again.

When the fog began, ever so slowly, to clear,

land, hilly and densely wooded, lay before them. The tops of the trees were still shawled in mist, which also hung like wispy tassels from branches. The sky was clotted with low cloud. One biggish house, half finished, and a few small huts, mean as slave shacks, freckled the shore. The place looked sulky, miserable. And the warship had vanished, gone on its way.

For a moment Rachel felt really lonely and forlorn. But then she spied Titan waiting with throngs of other Negroes on the lip of the small harbour into which they sailed. Titan was immense, head and shoulders above everyone else. As he came into sight, looming like a great ghost out of the icy gloom, he pulled off his cap and whooped it round in circles to greet them. Mamma squeezed Rachel's hand. She was so thrilled to catch sight of his big familiar face after all these months.

"He's got a new hat . . . an' new trousers too," she cried with delight as he stepped out of the crowd. "This mus' be a rich place and no mistake.

There mus' be more to it than what we're seein'."

"This here's Birchtown," sneered one of the deckhands. "What you see is what you get. Shelburne is just around the bay a piece. A prettier little new-town you'll never clap eyes on. But that's for whites. This here's your getting-off place. The Nigra stop, you might say, with emphasis on the 'stop.' Git your bundles together."

Rachel didn't move. It made no difference where they were. Everybody despised Negroes.

"Understand me, girl?"

"Oh, yessuh."

"Then what you staring at?"

"Nothing, suh." She picked up her bundle and balanced it on her head. It contained her blanket and some worsted stockings given to her on the boat.

"Home," thought Rachel. "Like it or not, this is it. I guess I'd better get used to it."

CHAPTER N.º 3

"Is one of them huts along the shore goin'
to be our house?" Mamma asked Titan, after the
three of them had greeted one another
thoroughly. Rachel had told Titan of their
new surname, and Mamma had admired his hat.

"Not exactly," he said, hoisting his family's
bundles over his shoulder and drawing Mamma
and Rachel away from the crowds.

Titan told them that he'd met every ship for the
past three months. He must have been hopeful,
thought Rachel, then despairing, of ever seeing his

13

wife and stepdaughter again. But as always, he didn't have much to say. He never used five words when one would do, never used one when he could get by with silence. Rachel remembered with a shock how close-mouthed he was. She would have to learn him all over again.

"Well, where is our house then?" she asked, glancing around. There was no place for a home, surely, not in this mess of forest and great grey boulders.

Titan said nothing, just turned and loped up the nearest hill, his long, badly worn shoes making no mark on the uneven, frosty ground. He couldn't run because of his missing toes, but he sure could walk fast. Mamma and Rachel had a hard time keeping up with him.

Rachel still felt just as dizzy as she'd been on the boat, with the land refusing to stay in place. It wobbled and rose up under her feet, almost tripping her. "I need to get my land legs," she thought. "And I must get shoes."

The soles of her feet were red and peeling, toes burning. She'd never worn footwear, never been

The three of them greeted one
another thoroughly. Rachel
told Titan of their new
surname, and Mamma admired
his hat.

given any. In the past her greatest fear had been snakebite as she'd darted to the rice fields carrying messages from the massa to the slave driver. She had had to be quick to spy out that fast, evil coil in the grass. Now, although she refused to voice her complaints aloud, she needed shoes desperately, but for a very different reason. She was afraid her toes were going to freeze, maybe even drop off, and the last thing in the world she wanted was for her feet to look like Titan's. When the family finally reached their new house, she'd put on her new stockings. But not out in this wilderness, with no shoes to protect them. They'd be ruined in no time.

"Here," said Titan at last, dropping the bundles and taking off his hat to scratch his round, curly-haired head. He was standing next to a large pit about three feet deep. A couple of wooden boxes, a mat, a blanket, and some tools were spread untidily below him. A cracked china cup and jug sat on one of the boxes.

Rachel nudged forward till her toes curled

over the edge of the hole. To think Titan had been sleeping in this awful place. It was so small, like an animal's lair, and it reeked of earth, sea . . . and something worse. She sniffed. Mould, maybe. Bones. The smell reminded her of dead things, and she drew back quickly.

"Are you thinkin' of buryin' someone?" asked Mamma, staring into the pit wretchedly. "We can't live there. I ain't goin' to have my bebby there. I'm needin' a cradle for him, not a grave." She went quiet for a moment, then moaned, "Titan, where are your wits? You must've lost 'em when you crossed over the wide ocean." Sitting down on a large white rock, she fished a blanket out of her bundle, wrapped it around her, and began to sway back and forth.

Mamma was right. This hole was just like the one the Negroes dug at night back home to bury their dead in. Cleared of the boxes, it might hold two coffins, three in a pinch, certainly no more. Three. One for each of them. Rachel shuddered at the thought, tried not to cry as the first stinging tears spiked through her lids.

"We got to build up the sides with wood, maybe another two foot, sling a roof over. It'll do us for winter, keep the snow out. In spring the white bosses'll give us our land and we'll build a proper house. Others roundabout are doing the same thing."

This was a long speech for Titan, and he seemed worn out with the effort of pushing it through his teeth. But as he pointed away up the hill, Rachel could see he was right. Dark wisps of smoke spiralled up from what looked like holes in the forest floor. People, perhaps other children, were down underground, a whole village of them, living in the dark. Well, if they could do it, so could she.

"How can I help, Titan?" she asked brightly, swallowing the tears that had run down the back of her nose into her throat. "I'm big and strong as most grown-ups. I can fetch wood. I can hew it if need be. Maybe we can get some kind of a roof up before nightfall."

"Good for you," was his only reply. And for a

fleeting moment he sounded like the white man on the ship who had written down their names.

"Seems a sad thing," Mamma remarked, "that you been here all this time buildin' houses for the white folk, but you ain't had time to build one for yoursel'." She got up and began to unpack the bundles, then bustled around starting to create a home for the three of them.

"That's the way of it, sure enough," said Titan. He slid into the hole to fetch his axe to cut wood with, and Rachel scrambled down too. It was only then that she noticed how he'd lined the earthen sides with ferns and pine branches to try to make things snugger for them.

Much, much later, while gathering moss to chink the spaces in the low wooden walls of their new hut, Rachel would suddenly remember Titan saying something about keeping the snow out. What was snow?

CHAPTER N°. 4

No one was talking in their dark home.
Titan hardly ever spoke anyway. There was little
work to be had in the frigid weather, and he
spent his time trying to fit his large body more
comfortably into their small space. Mamma,
dragging herself around and close to birthing the
baby, had all but stopped talking too.

"Winter has frozen our tongues too cold to
wag," she crabbed when Rachel remarked on
how quiet it was. "And don' you go naggin' me,
girl. Least you can stan' up in here. I got to walk

around with legs or neck bent all the time, and Titan can't stan' up at all. This ain't the house I been wishin' for. This ain't the kinda life I been wishin' for, neither. Free Nigras, indeed."

It was bitterly cold, but Rachel was glad to get out, climbing through the trap door in the sloping roof and sliding down its icy surface to the ground before someone could call her back. She needed to be outside, to be free of her family for a while, even though the glacial weather would drive her back almost immediately. It was so cramped indoors, and any talk was a complaint.

But Mamma was right, she could see that. At least on the plantation they had always been warm, often too warm, with their bellies part full, even if only with yams or broken grains of rice. Here they were freezing every time they stepped out, half frozen when they stepped in, and their stomachs growled day and night like dogs howling at the door. And all they had by way of supplies was some cornmeal with white wriggly worms in it and a bit of what the British called treacle. It was just molasses by another name.

"Not near enough to keep body and soul together," Mamma would grumble, as she cooked the cornmeal over the fire. "Only the worms are gettin' fat. How we s'posed to live out the winter like this?"

Rachel moved clear of the middens near the cabin and took a deep breath of frosty air. Ice and ashes, refreshing after the stink inside. Could it possibly be better to be a slave than a free girl? She was beginning to have worrying, disloyal thoughts.

Snow lay all over the rocky ground, had been there for days, so deep that it caught the weird imprint of her bare foot with its flattish heel and sole. She took another step and admired it, then skipped several times and did an untidy handspring. Her skirt flew up and breath streamed out of her in a white fog.

She'd known right away what snow was as soon as it had begun to drift down in fat, wet flakes. She relished its taste on her tongue and its tingle around her toes. The earth was softer to walk on, and she could draw pictures that stayed until there was a fresh fall. Now she made lacy patterns with her fingernail, took a stick and traced around her feet, then kneeled and wrote over and over the letters that she knew.

"That's an S, and that's a P," she said out loud, trying to spell "Sparrow" the way the captain had spelled it in his book. "I'll have to go inside soon. My feet are like blocks of ice. I can't feel them any more." She stopped for a moment to rub them. "That's a . . . oh dear, I recognize it, but I don't know what it's called. How am I going to learn to read if I don't even know my alphabet? And how am I ever going to be truly free if I can't read?" Rachel had heard another slave say that one time on the plantation, took it to mean that if you could read you could pull yourself up by your bootstraps if you had any, make a better life for yourself.

Something stirred behind a tree, and a faint,

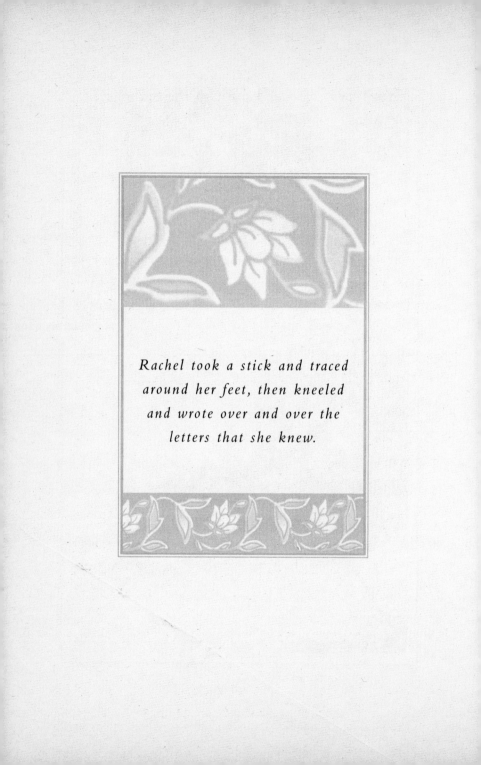

*Rachel took a stick and traced
around her feet, then kneeled
and wrote over and over the
letters that she knew.*

silvery spray cascaded through the branches.

"Who's there?" Rachel called. Her voice sounded strangely high in the snowy woods, where the air was so sharp and clear that nothing seemed quite real.

"Who's there, I say?" Was it an animal or a person?

A slight rustle was quickly followed by a flurry of movement. Rachel was almost sure she saw a long black braid fly out and slap across a trunk. It disappeared in a flash. Afterwards there was only silence and stillness. And a row of small, light footprints among the birches.

"It was a person," sighed Rachel, not sure whether to be pleased or scared. "A child, I think, a girl." There *were* children in Birchtown, other Negro children, but she saw them only rarely. Many were shoeless, like herself, and it was too wintry most of the time for them to venture out.

"But that wasn't a Nigra child," she decided suddenly.

When the words were out, singing in the cold

air, she felt an awful wretchedness, a splash of loneliness. Whoever the child was, Rachel needed her company. But although longing to follow the prints till she found their owner, she realized it would be far too dangerous. Slowly, regretfully, she climbed up the roof to the trap door, slid inside, and dragged her stockings over her numb feet.

By Titan's reckoning, it was now Christmas, give or take a day. He said as much, surprising Mamma and Rachel with the sound of his voice. Then he set eightpence down on one of the boxes, his wages for a recent day's work. Everybody grinned, but a few minutes afterwards, Mamma put down the spoon she was stirring the supper with, leaned her arm against the wall, and groaned.

"Christmas, eh? Well, I think we're jus' about to get a present. Rachel, you better go fetch Nanna Jacklin, that ole bent lady with the scratchy voice. You know where she lives?"

"Yes, Mamma. By the shore, in the hut with three glass windows."

"Tell her to hurry. The bebby's comin', an' I need a woman with me."

Rachel was off and running. The forest was dense with snow, falling so thickly that she could barely see the outlines of trees. She moved rapidly from pine to pine, hugging each as she went, trying to keep her balance in the buffeting wind.

What was that? Her imagination must be playing tricks with her. A shadowy presence seemed to sway and shift, matching her progress step for step. She stopped, digging in her toes. It stopped. She started down the hill again.

Someone ran beside her.

Rachel's heart lunged into her throat. She turned and screamed, her voice hoarse with fear. "Who's there? Tell me at once. You followed me the other day, too."

Nothing. The wind roared.

"Tell me. Show yourself now."

Still nothing.

"If you don't come over *here*," shouted Rachel, trying to sound her bravest, "I'm going to come over *there* and fetch you. Just see if I don't."

There was a slight movement. At first she thought it was a bear, a huge winter bear, emerging from the veil of snow, and she almost died of fright. That would teach her to go yelling at strangers in the forest. But as it came closer she realized that this was a child of about her own age, an Indian girl cloaked in animal skins. The girl had long black hair which, unbraided today, blew out behind her, and she gripped something firmly in her slender hands.

"For you," she murmured in a gentle voice that nonetheless carried across the wind. She held out a pair of bright, soft shoes, high-ankled and beautifully beaded and quilled.

"Micmac moccasins," she whispered. "I wanted

to give them before. I saw how cold you were, but I was too afraid."

Rachel slipped them on, stunned that anyone, never mind a perfect stranger, should give her anything. It was blissful, the way the fur lining comforted her frozen feet.

After admiring the shoes and their perfect fit for several moments, she remembered her manners and looked up to say thank you. The Indian girl had vanished.

CHAPTER *N*.º 5

Nanna Jacklin brought her grandson Corey
with her to the Sparrow hut. A very little boy
with filthy feet and hands, he was not above asking a bale of questions while his grandmother
helped Mamma through her labour.

"Where you get them boots?" he asked Rachel.

"None of your business." He was far too young
to be a playmate to her.

"Why your daddy got two toes missing?"

Titan was creeping around barefoot, trying to
be useful.

"He's not my daddy, he's my stepdaddy."

"Where your real daddy, then?" Corey's hair looked as though no one had ever brushed it. It stood out in matted spikes around his head.

"He was sold away from the Roberts' place, where we lived." Rachel replied tersely. She moved as far away from Corey as she could in the cramped pit, but he came after her.

"Why he sold?"

"This is the last answer I'm ever going to give you. D'you understand?"

"Yessum."

"Well, then. Because he was a strong Nigra slave and someone offered the massa an armload of money for him."

"So why your *stepdaddy* got two toes missing?"

"That's it. I told you before. I've no answers left," snapped Rachel, much annoyed.

"Pleasum?"

"Oh, very well. But nothing else, never, ever. The massa cut them off after the first time he ran away. It slowed him up some, but it didn't stop him, else he couldn't have brought us here."

Titan heard and grinned. Then Mamma cried out and put an end to all the talk. Titan went over to her, holding her hand and pushing her hair back from the livid scar on her forehead.

"Bebby here," yelled Nanna Jacklin a few moments later. "A great big boy, jus' like his father, but he got all his toes! Fingers too, ten of 'em, ripplin' like corn in the field." She wrapped him in a bit of torn cloth and handed him to his mother.

"Where you get them shoes?" whispered Mamma hoarsely, heaving herself up on one shoulder.

"From an Indian girl, Mamma. She gave them to me."

"Well, you watch them Indians. They not our kind," she warned before sinking down again. "You need other Nigras to know where you are."

Rachel frowned and snuggled farther into her moccasins. Nanna Jacklin gathered her things and took Corey home.

The new baby had very pale skin, which made Rachel wince because it kept reminding her of the maggots in the cornmeal. But right away, everyone else loved the ugly creature, whose name was Jem. Mamma had decided beforehand she'd call a son that. A daughter, which was what Rachel had been hoping for, would have been Phebe.

"And you will be a bright gem, sure as the sun shines," Titan would say, enveloping the baby in his strong arms. "Maybe a hard diamond when you're grown."

Titan was so proud of his son that he'd taken to talking to him. As for Mamma, instead of her usual bossiness and complaints, there was laughter, and she crooned to the baby as she suckled him. At night she and Titan cuddled up with Jem between them, to keep the little mite warm. Rachel, who still couldn't understand what all the fuss was about, felt especially left out when no one even bothered to cook her a meal or admire her moccasins. She boiled her own corn-meal sullenly, spooning in more than her rightful share of treacle.

"Lookee here, Sukey. He's smiling at me," exclaimed Titan one day with great excitement as the baby displayed his little pink tongue and gums.

"Every grin gum don't mean smile," Mamma replied, smiling herself. "He mus' have the wind."

"Give him to me. I'll burp him." Rachel held her arms out. "I'm trying to love you, baby, I really am. But just look at you." She held Jem close to the fire so she could examine him properly. "Your skin is much too light, not Nigra skin at all, and your eyes are so blue I can see clear through them to midnight. They should be brown, boy."

"A bebby's jus' like cornbread not full-baked." Mamma had an explanation for everything.

"Well, he looks awful. And he sounds even worse," Rachel went on, as the baby began to squall. "Crying all the livelong day and driving me crazy."

"Hush, girl. You were jus' the same. You'll like him well enough when he's grown. He's gonna be a good frien' to you." Taking Jem, Mamma put him to her breast, closing her eyes as he sucked. She seemed to be shutting her daughter out completely.

"I don't need him. I already have a friend." Rachel muttered rebelliously. She was thinking of the Indian girl with the fly-away hair. She'd have to go out and find her. Anything to get away from that baby. They should put him in the rubbish.

CHAPTER N⁰ 6

She looked everywhere, but it seemed that the Indian girl didn't want to be found. Rachel watched for her footprints in vain, often with Corey trailing along. He seemed to have attached himself to her, and although she did her best to ignore him, he rarely fell back or stopped asking questions.

One morning Rachel went so far afield that she came upon a small town. She had a shawl on that she'd made from a bit of woven cloth, left over when Mamma tore up an old blanket to make wraps for Jem. Drawing it around her tightly, she peeked through the trees at the glint of brooding bay, with its dense cluster of wooden houses and banked-up snow.

"This must be Shelburne," she thought, remembering, with a small shudder, the scornful words of the crewman on the boat. Shelburne was a white town, not like the "Nigra stop" where Rachel lived.

Shelburne, as the man had hinted, looked nothing like Birchtown. The houses were bigger, for a start, some almost as big as the massa's house on the plantation. Many had barns and outhouses, and all but a few appeared to be brand new. In fact, most were so new they seemed barely finished, and others, scattered along long, straight streets, were still timber skeletons. Rachel guessed that they would be completed come spring. Maybe Titan would have a hand in the work and he could collect some more eightpences.

Despite the shin-deep snow, the place was

thronged with people going about their business. Most of them were white, but Rachel could see two Negroes, one shaking out a mat, the other pulling a heavy load along a snowy street. She felt encouraged to sneak down among them, almost as if their presence made her invisible.

She was still on the outskirts of the town, still among the tall pines, thinking how wonderful it must be to live there, with proper beds and fire-places, with chimneys and front doors and stores nearby full (as she imagined) of food and fabrics, when a shrill, scathing voice cut in on her thoughts.

"Hey, Nigra. Whose Nigra are you?"

She turned abruptly, almost knocking over a tall, well-dressed white boy.

"I'm nobody's Nigra. I'm free," she said haughtily, drawing herself up to her full height and then adding an inch or two by standing on tiptoe. Pulling her shawl even more tightly around her shoulders, she scrunched down hard on her heels, wheeled around as fast as she could without falling, and began to move away as rapidly as possible.

But he darted by, and a second later he was standing in front of her again, tossing back his light brown hair.

"You'll go when I tell you to, and not before. I said, whose Nigra are you? Answer me properly this time."

Rachel had long understood that there were two ways of saying "Nigra." When Mamma and other Negroes said it, it was soft and open, like part of a lullaby. In some white men's mouths, though, it was harsh, painful, sounding like an insult. This boy, with his careless swagger and sharp, high voice, made it into the nastiest insult of all. He made it sound as though she were an animal.

"I told you, I'm free. I don't have a massa. My stepdaddy joined the British army and we were all released from slavery."

His eyes were ice blue. "Why, you stupid girl. You're one of those filthy urchins from Birchtown. How dare you come here and flaunt yourself among respectable white people?"

Rachel moved forward again, trying to get past him, but he stuck out his foot in its brass-buckled shoe and tripped her. She went sprawling.

"That'll teach you," he crowed. "I go to school and I know everything. You, on the other hand, you skinny great scarecrow of a Nigra, are ignorant as dirt. Now get out of here."

Rachel would have gone, would have been glad to. That's what she'd been taught all her life: to swallow the taunts and mockery of white people, even if, like now, she was burning with so much anger that she saw red splotches every time she blinked. But as she pushed her wrists down into the spiky crystals of snow to heave herself up and away, she spotted Corey hunched behind a tree. The little monster must have followed her all the way from Birchtown . . . without asking her a single question! No wonder she hadn't realized he was there.

Now, no matter what she'd been taught, no matter how dangerous it was to answer back, there was no way she was about to act the coward. Even if Corey was a little nobody who crouched shivering in the snow, he reminded her, very uncomfortably, of herself.

She scrambled up and glared directly into the tall boy's face. He might be as stuck up as a lord, he might think he knew everything, but there was one thing he didn't know: he had a thin stream of snot running from his nose to the dent in the middle of his upper lip. As it gathered there in a little pool, glistening and slimy as a snail track, somehow it changed everything. Why, under his fine clothes and his fancy shoes, she thought with a kind of frightened glee, he was just the same as everyone else.

"I'm not stupid and I'm not filthy," she said in a stately voice. "I may be poor but I'm as clever and good as you. Probably cleverer and better, in fact."

The boy was so shocked that for a scant second the wind went out of him, and his shoulders slumped. Rachel used that second to push her

Rachel tried to get past him, but
he stuck out his foot in its
brass-buckled shoe and tripped
her. She went sprawling. Corey
hunched behind a tree.

advantage. "And I mayn't go to school, but I can read and write anyhow," she said proudly.

"Nigras can't write," he blustered. "It's not allowed. None of our slaves can write."

So his family owned slaves. No wonder he behaved the way he did. And how sad that even in Nova Scotia there were still Negroes who had to obey a massa.

Rachel picked up a stick. The boy smashed it viciously out of her hand.

"I wasn't going to hit you, only show I can write," she remarked sadly. She knelt down in the snow and traced out R for Rachel with her index finger. Then she wrote S, P, A (she still didn't know what that letter was called, though she knew its sound), R, R, O, W. "That's my name," she said. "Rachel Sparrow."

"What a stupid name. This is mine," he said proudly. "Nathan A. Crowley." He picked up the stick he'd struck from her hand and wrote the letters in the snow. Now she knew how to say the A letter.

"What does the A stand for?" she asked.

"Archelaus," he said smugly. "After my grand-father."

He was now writing something else, a long something that was taking him such a deal of time that his tongue protruded with the effort and he panted his foggy breath into the air.

"What does that say?" she asked, trying desperately to commit the snow writing to memory.

"It says: 'Get out of here if you know what's good for you,'" sneered Nathan. "I knew you couldn't read."

"Oh, but I can now." She smiled. "Look." She repeated his words as she traced her finger under what he'd written. "You just taught me how. Thank you, Nathan Archelaus Crowley."

She dodged him and whirled away, laughing. Behind the tree, she could hear little Corey clapping.

Mamma was sick, coughing and moaning,
tossing on the two boxes stuck together she
called a bed. Titan was so worried that he went
to fetch Nanna Jacklin.

"She's worn out with the bebby and the cold
and the bad food. I ain't even got my herbs here
in this God-forsaken place. I'm sorry, Titan, but
there ain't nothin' I can give her." The old
woman shook her head and went home.

Mamma wasn't even well enough to feed Jem.
The baby cried listlessly until Rachel thought to

dip a piece of cloth in treacle and give it to him to suck. But on the second night of Mamma's illness, he started to cough too, a harsh, brittle cough that sounded like dry twigs breaking. At dawn he was still hacking.

For a moment Rachel felt a tiny triumph. "Now you know what it's like to be hungry and miserable, like the rest of us," she thought. Then she felt ashamed, a deep, dark shame that sat in the pit of her belly and wouldn't shift. Jem was really sick, really starving, poor little helpless thing. It was all her fault, she knew it was, for wanting to throw him away.

She made up her mind. "I'm taking him outside, Titan. All the smoke and cinders in here can't be good for his chest."

"Cold air'll make him even sicker," said Titan.

"We have to do something. He'll die if we don't. He hasn't eaten for days, and now this."

Titan barely nodded before turning back to Mamma, who had broken out in a sweat and was trying to throw off her blanket. He was exhausted,

Rachel could see that. He moved slow as a land-locked turtle to push Mamma's covers back over her. The whites of his eyes had turned yellow, and his eyelids sagged at the corners. Rachel felt sorry for him, sorry for them all, including herself. She was frightened, too, that Mamma might never recover. But she had to look after the baby. Mamma would expect her to.

After wrapping Jem in two scraps of blanket, she climbed through the trap door and slid outside with him. The sky was fine and clear, still blue-black down by the water, hazy pink through the pine trees to the east. She sat on a big flat rock and talked to him as he lay in the circle of her arms.

"I'm sorry, baby, I really am. I didn't mean for you to get sick. Now take a few breaths of this good air into your lungs and you'll feel a whole lot better."

Jem coughed.

"You must be feeling pretty bad. You haven't had any milk for a while. Now how would it be if I gave you something to take the edge off your thirst?"

Jem stared up at her with his strange, wise eyes, and Rachel suddenly felt he knew more than Mamma and Titan, more than Nathan Archelaus Crowley, more than anyone in the whole wide world. Perhaps he even knew how much she'd wanted him gone. Babies often looked that way, though. She'd noticed that with the missus' children. But by the time they were two, judging by the way they behaved, they'd forgotten everything.

She needed to try to love Jem, to think of him as a member of her family, no matter how hard it was. She bent forward and scooped up a few small speckles of fresh snow, rolled them together between thumb and forefinger, then thrust the miniature snowball she'd made into the baby's mouth. Jem sucked on it eagerly.

"Here's some more. It's just water, really, but it seems to be doing you a power of good."

She fed him till he wouldn't suck any longer,

then sat quietly with him, watching the red sun thrust its way into the early sky.

"It's not that you've done anything wrong," she whispered at last. "Not really. It's just that you're taking my place with Mamma and Titan. I don't feel as if I belong any more. And they're all I've got. I don't have anyone else to belong *to*."

There was a flicker behind a tree. She wondered whether it might be Corey again, but she was suddenly too exhausted to go find out. Her eyelids were so heavy that she had trouble keeping them open. She began to drift, dream back her old landscape in Charlestown: grey moss dripping like dusty spiderwebs from a giant oak, intense heat, the song-like splash of the Cooper River.

She awoke with a start, half frozen. It was full daylight, and the Indian girl was sitting beside her. The girl had taken Jem into her own lap and was crooning to him in a strange soft language. The baby had his thumb in his mouth. His eyes were shut and he'd stopped coughing.

"Cold air is good for babies' coughs," the girl said gently. "It cleanses their lungs, makes their little bodies healthy again. My family have always known this. You did the right thing."

Rachel rubbed her eyes to make sure she wasn't dreaming. "My mamma is sick too," she confided to the girl. "I'm afraid she'll die. What can we do for her?"

"I'll fetch my aunt. If anyone will know what to do, she will. She's a healer."

Carefully, the girl handed Jem back to Rachel and, turning, sped off through the woods.

CHAPTER N:o 8

Many weeks later, Rachel took Jem outside
again. Things were going well. The Indian girl's
aunt had arrived right away with a great flourish,
a good deal of harrumphing, and a skin bag full
of Micmac medicine. She'd stayed till Mamma
was on the mend, and now the two women,
although still a little wary of each other, were
almost friends. Rachel had even heard them
laughing together.

Jem was thriving, and Titan was earning a
whole shilling every day as a carpenter over in

Shelburne. That meant better meals and warmer clothing. Best of all, Rachel and the Indian girl, Ann-Marie, had become firm friends too.

Ann-Marie had shown Rachel how to chew up tiny bits of food and spit them into Jem's mouth so he wouldn't starve.

"Ugh! I feel like a mother bird feeding my baby a worm," said Rachel, dismayed. But Ann-Marie's trick worked. Jem grew strong, even though Mamma was too sick to nurse him. And as she took care of him, Rachel couldn't help but come to love him. She stroked his little head and sang to him. Sometimes she even thought of him as her baby.

Loving her brother was a precious gift, a gift that Ann-Marie had given her. What could she do for the Indian girl in return? All she had were words, with not too many stories to shape them into. Finally, she decided: she would tell Ann-Marie how they'd all run away from the plantation.

There had been many quilts in the massa's house. Every quilt, with its different pattern

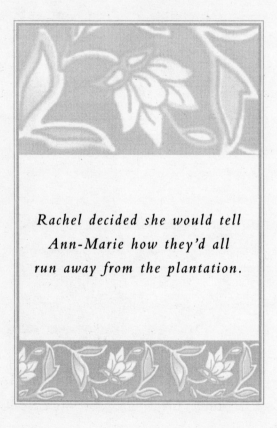

Rachel decided she would tell Ann-Marie how they'd all run away from the plantation.

meant something important to the slaves. If Mamma was making the missus' bed and hung a certain quilt out of the window to air, it meant "stay away." Another quilt meant "massa fighting mad enough to whup someone." The day the Sparrows left, Mamma had hung out the most important quilt of all. It told Titan to come in from his work early. They were going to escape, run to the British army for protection.

This story led to another—how Mamma had got her scar. How the massa had been beating her when an edge of the lash had whipped round her face, almost taking out an eye. Mamma had vowed then, Rachel told Ann-Marie, that her family would be free some day.

"Lots of Nigras have scars like that, but Mamma was more shamed than most to be beaten. And it was for such a little thing. Taking a piece of bread from his table to give to her small hungry girl at home. That was me," Rachel said with surprise, as if she'd never fully realized it before. "She wanted to give the bread to me.

She told me once, but now she never speaks of it. It's a kind of hurting secret she carries with her."

"I'll never speak of it either," Ann-Marie promised, her dark eyes wide with shock.

For a while Rachel was scared that she had made a mistake in telling her friend. But she had nothing to worry about. In sharing Mamma's secret, the two girls became closer than ever.

Rachel was waiting for Ann-Marie now. She spread a blanket over a dry patch of earth and set Jem down on it. He stared up into the pines and waved his legs and arms in the air.

The trees smelled wonderful, fresh and faintly perfumed. They stole the stink of the pit cabin out of Rachel's nose. The snow was almost gone, slowly disappearing even from the dark places in the forest and the high places on the hills. There was a mildness to the air she hadn't experienced since coming to Birchtown.

"How you spell my name?" It was Corey, of course—Corey with his filthy feet, matted hair, and endless questions. He came whenever Nanna

Jacklin was gone about her business, and he still stuck to Rachel like a burr.

She moved to shoo him away, then changed her mind. She ought to be patient with him. It would be good practice for taking care of Jem as he got older.

"C, O, R—" She wrote the letters in the dirt by the blanket. "I'm not sure of the rest."

"Corey. That my daddy's name, too."

Rachel felt a stinging sorrow. A short time back she'd found out that Corey's daddy and mamma were both dead. They'd been caught escaping from their massa and shot. That's why Corey lived with Nanna Jacklin.

"Listen, Corey, I'm going to find out for you. Everybody should know how to spell their name. In fact, everybody should know how to read and write. I just have to figure how to get all that knowing out of Nathan Crowley's head and into mine. He's easy to fool, and I'll do it. Then I'll be able to teach you everything you need to become a smart, free man." She sat back, very pleased with herself. How difficult could it be?

Baby Jem smiled at her, a proper smile. Mamma had said he wasn't full-baked when he was born, but now he was browning nicely. And his eyes were starting to deepen to a lovely copper. Give him another month and he'd have proper Nigra eyes, just like Rachel's. He really did belong to their family. Mamma was right.

Rachel cooed at the baby. He cooed back.

Tufts of bright-green grass and yellow shoots were pushing out of the earth to gleam in the watery sun. A bird sang somewhere far off. Spring was coming, and Titan had promised them a new house come spring. She wondered idly if it would have glass windows, like Nanna Jacklin's and the rich people's houses in Shelburne. And whether there would be stores nearby, where she could buy herself a new shift and a proper petticoat.

"Why the snow melt?" nagged Corey, impossible as ever. He was digging in the hard earth with a pointed stick and looked dirtier than a chimney sweep.

"Because the weather's warmer, because the sun's out, because spring's coming, because winter's gone, because God is rewarding us, because, oh, I don't know." Rachel was laughing.

Jem, catching her eye, began to laugh too, a deep, throaty gurgle. As his mouth opened, she caught sight of two pearly buds—his first teeth! Whooping with joy, she jumped up, caught Corey by the hand so his stick went sailing into the air, and whirled him round till they were both giddy.

"Hello," called Ann-Marie, coming up the hill in time to watch them spin. "You are having a good time."

"Yes, we are," Rachel shouted. "That's because I've got spring in me today and I'm happy. I'm a free Nigra. A free Nigra in Nova Scotia. I'm going to learn to read and write whole sentences and I'm going to teach Corey how to spell his name."

"Good for you," Ann Marie replied, smiling.

Rachel went to fetch Jem. She lifted him high

so that he could see the tops of the wide-branched apple trees close by the shore.

"This is going to be our home, baby," Rachel resolved. "Here at the Nigra stop in Birchtown. We live here, we'll always live here, and I don't want to see Charlestown, that horrid slave place, ever again. I'll make sure you never see it either."

And she meant what she said, every word of it.

ACKNOWLEDGEMENTS

MANY THANKS TO MY FAMILY AND FRIENDS;

TO COREY GUY, AND TO CLARA AND EARNESTINE OF THE

JACKLYN FAMILY, ALL DESCENDANTS OF THE

ORIGINAL BLACK LOYALISTS;

TO LAIRD NIVEN, THE ARCHAEOLOGIST OF THE BIRCHTOWN SITE,

AND TO PATRICIA CLARK OF SENECA COLLEGE, WHO WERE BOTH

IMMENSELY HELPFUL;

TO LEONA TRAINER, MY WONDERFUL AGENT;

TO BARBARA BERSON, MY TERRIFIC EDITOR;

TO CINDY KANTOR, WHO BROUGHT THE IDEA FOR

THE SERIES TO PENGUIN;

AND

TO BOOKFRIENDS, WHO ARE ALWAYS AN AMAZING SOURCE OF

SUPPORT AND GOOD HUMOUR.

Dear Reader,

Did you enjoy reading this Our Canadian Girl adventure? Write us and tell us what you think! We'd love to hear about your favourite parts, which characters you like best, and even whom else you'd like to see stories about. Maybe you'd like to read an adventure with one of Our Canadian Girls that happened in your hometown—fifty, a hundred years ago or more!

Send your letters to:
>Our Canadian Girl
>c/o Penguin Canada
>10 Alcorn Avenue, Suite 300
>Toronto, ON M4V 3B2

Be sure to check your bookstore for more books in the Our Canadian Girl series. There are some ready for you right now, and more are on their way.

We look forward to hearing from you!

Sincerely,
>*Barbara Berson*
>PENGUIN BOOKS CANADA

P.S. Don't forget to visit us online at www.ourcanadiangirl.ca—there are some other girls you should meet!

Canada's

1608
Samuel de Champlain establishes the first fortified trading post at Quebec.

1759
The British defeat the French in the Battle of the Plains of Abraham.

1812
The United States declares war against Canada.

1845
The expedition of Sir John Franklin to the Arctic ends when the ship is frozen in the pack ice; the fate of its crew remains a mystery.

1869
Louis Riel leads his Métis followers in the Red River Rebellion.

1871
British Columbia joins Canada.

1755
The British expel the entire French population of Acadia (today's Maritime provinces), sending them into exile.

1776
The 13 Colonies revolt against Britain, and the Loyalists flee to Canada.

1837
Calling for responsible government, the Patriotes, following Louis-Joseph Papineau, rebel in Lower Canada; William Lyon Mackenzie leads the uprising in Upper Canada.

1867
New Brunswick, Nova Scotia and the United Province of Canada come together in Confederation to form the Dominion of Canada.

1870
Manitoba joins Canada. The Northwest Territories become an official territory of Canada.

1783
Rachel

Timeline

1885
At Craigellachie, British Columbia, the last spike is driven to complete the building of the Canadian Pacific Railway.

1898
The Yukon Territory becomes an official territory of Canada.

1914
Britain declares war on Germany, and Canada, because of its ties to Britain, is at war too.

1918
As a result of the Wartime Elections Act, the women of Canada are given the right to vote in federal elections.

1945
World War II ends conclusively with the dropping of atomic bombs on Hiroshima and Nagasaki.

1873
Prince Edward Island joins Canada.

1896
Gold is discovered on Bonanza Creek, a tributary of the Klondike River.

1905
Alberta and Saskatchewan join Canada.

1917
In the Halifax harbour, two ships collide, causing an explosion that leaves more than 1,600 dead and 9,000 injured.

1939
Canada declares war on Germany seven days after war is declared by Britain and France.

1949
Newfoundland, under the leadership of Joey Smallwood, joins Canada.

1885
Marie-Claire

1896
Emily

1917
Penelope